NOTE

`Twas the Night was written by Dr. Clement Clarke Moore, probably in 1823; but since it was first published anonymously, and not credited to him until many years later, the champions of a rival author have found it possible to advance their claims.

The rival is Henry Livingston Jr., whose descendants claim a family tradition establishing their ancestor as the author. But actual proof of his authorship is lacking, and Arthur N. Hosking, who published a small volume on the subject, has confirmed the authorship of Clement Clarke Moore.

The poem was first printed, anonymously, in the *Troy Sentinel* of December 23, 1823. It was credited to Moore in the *New York Book of Poetry*, 1837. Moore acknowledged his authorship in his *Poems*, 1844. And during the hundred years since that time the children of America have taken over the poem as their very own.

To:

From:

Cover Design: Amy Titcomb

`Twas the Night Before Christmas

By
Clement Moore

Illustrated by
Linda Hoffer

PETER PAUPER PRESS, INC.
WHITE PLAINS • NEW YORK

'Twas the night before Christmas,
    when all through the house
Not a creature was stirring,
    not even a mouse;
The stockings were hung
    by the chimney with care,
In hopes that St. Nicholas
    soon would be there;
The children were nestled
    all snug in their beds,
While visions of sugar-plums
    danced through their heads;

And Mamma in her 'kerchief,
    and I in my cap,
Had just settled our brains
    for a long winter's nap,
When out on the lawn
    there arose such a clatter,
I sprang from my bed
    to see what was the matter.
Away to the window
    I flew like a flash,
Tore open the shutters
    and threw up the sash.

The moon on the breast
of the new-fallen snow
Gave a lustre of mid-day
to objects below,
When, what to my wondering
eyes did appear,
But a miniature sleigh,
and eight tiny rein-deer,
With a little old driver
so lively and quick,
I knew in a moment
he must be St. Nick.
More rapid than eagles
his coursers they came,
And he whistled, and shouted,
and called them by name:
" Now, Dasher! now, Dancer!
now, Prancer and Vixen!

On, Comet! on, Cupid!
  on, Donder and Blixen!
To the top of the porch!
  to the top of the wall!
Now dash away! dash away!
  dash away, all!"
As leaves that before
  the wild hurricane fly,
When they meet with an obstacle,
  mount to the sky,
So up to the house-top
  the coursers they flew,
With the sleigh full of toys,
  and St. Nicholas too—
And then in a twinkling,
  I heard on the roof
The prancing and pawing
  of each little hoof.

As I drew in my head,
  and was turning around,
Down the chimney St. Nicholas
  came with a bound.
He was dressed all in fur,
  from his head to his foot,
And his clothes were all tarnished
  with ashes and soot;
A bundle of toys he had
  flung on his back,
And he looked like a peddler
  just opening his pack.

His eyes—how they twinkled!
  his dimples, how merry!
His cheeks were like roses,
  his nose like a cherry!
His droll little mouth
  was drawn up like a bow,
And the beard on his chin
  was as white as the snow;
The stump of a pipe
  he held tight in his teeth,
And the smoke it encircled
  his head like a wreath;
He had a broad face
  and a round little belly
That shook when he laughed,
  like a bowl full of jelly.

He was chubby and plump,
  a right jolly old elf,
And I laughed when I saw him
  in spite of myself;
A wink of his eye and
  a twist of his head
Soon gave me to know
  I had nothing to dread;
He spoke not a word, but
  went straight to his work,
And filled all the stockings;
  then turned with a jerk,
And laying his finger
  aside of his nose,
And giving a nod, up the
  chimney he rose.

He sprang to his sleigh,
*   to his team gave a whistle,*
And away they all flew
*   like the down of a thistle.*
But I heard him exclaim
*   ere he drove out of sight —*
"Happy Christmas to all
*   and to all a Good Night!"*